Linkoping University.
1980.05.200

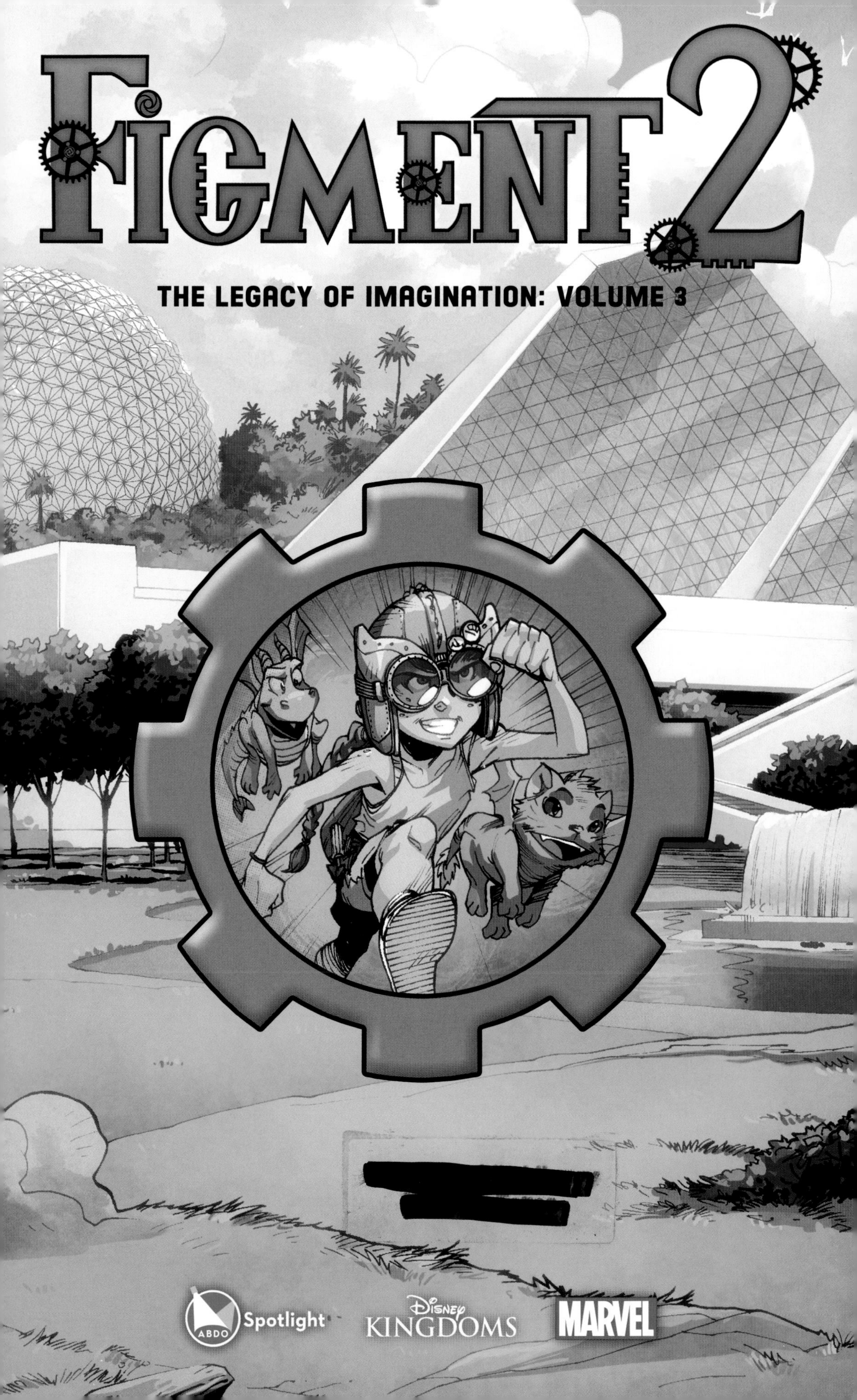

FIGMENT 2
THE LEGACY OF IMAGINATION: VOLUME 3
[redacted]
ABDO Spotlight
DISNEY KINGDOMS
MARVEL

ABDOPUBLISHING.COM

Reinforced library bound edition published in 2017 by Spotlight,
a division of ABDO, PO Box 398166, Minneapolis, Minnesota 55439.
Spotlight produces high-quality reinforced library bound editions for
schools and libraries. Published by agreement with Marvel Characters, Inc.

Printed in the United States of America, North Mankato, Minnesota.
092016
012017

THIS BOOK CONTAINS
RECYCLED MATERIALS

marvelkids.com
© 2016 MARVEL

Elements based on Figment © Disney.

PUBLISHER'S CATALOGING IN PUBLICATION DATA

Names: Zub, Jim, author. | Bachs, Ramon ; Beaulieu, Jean-Francois, illustrators.
Title: Figment 2 : The Legacy of Imagination / writer: Jim Zub ; art: Ramon Bachs
    ; Jean-Francois Beaulieu.
Description: Reinforced library bound edition. | Minneapolis, Minnesota : Spotlight,
    2017. | Series: Disney Kingdoms : Figment Set 2
Summary: After flying through a portal, Dreamfinder and Figment find themselves
    in the 21st century at the new Academy, but when a demonstration goes
    wrong, Dreamfinder transforms into the Doubtfinder, leaving Figment and
    Capri to free Dreamfinder before doubt can take over the world.
Identifiers: LCCN 2016941716 | ISBN 9781614795810 (volume 1) | ISBN
    9781614795827 (volume 2) | ISBN 9781614795834 (volume 3) | ISBN
    9781614795841 (volume 4) | ISBN 9781614795858 (volume 5)
Subjects: LCSH: Disney (Fictitious characters)--Juvenile fiction. | Adventure and
    adventurers--Juvenile fiction. | Comic books, strips, etc.--Juvenile fiction. |
    Graphic novels--Juvenile fiction.
Classification: DDC 741.5--dc23
LC record available at https://lccn.loc.gov/2016941716

Spotlight

A Division of ABDO
abdopublishing.com

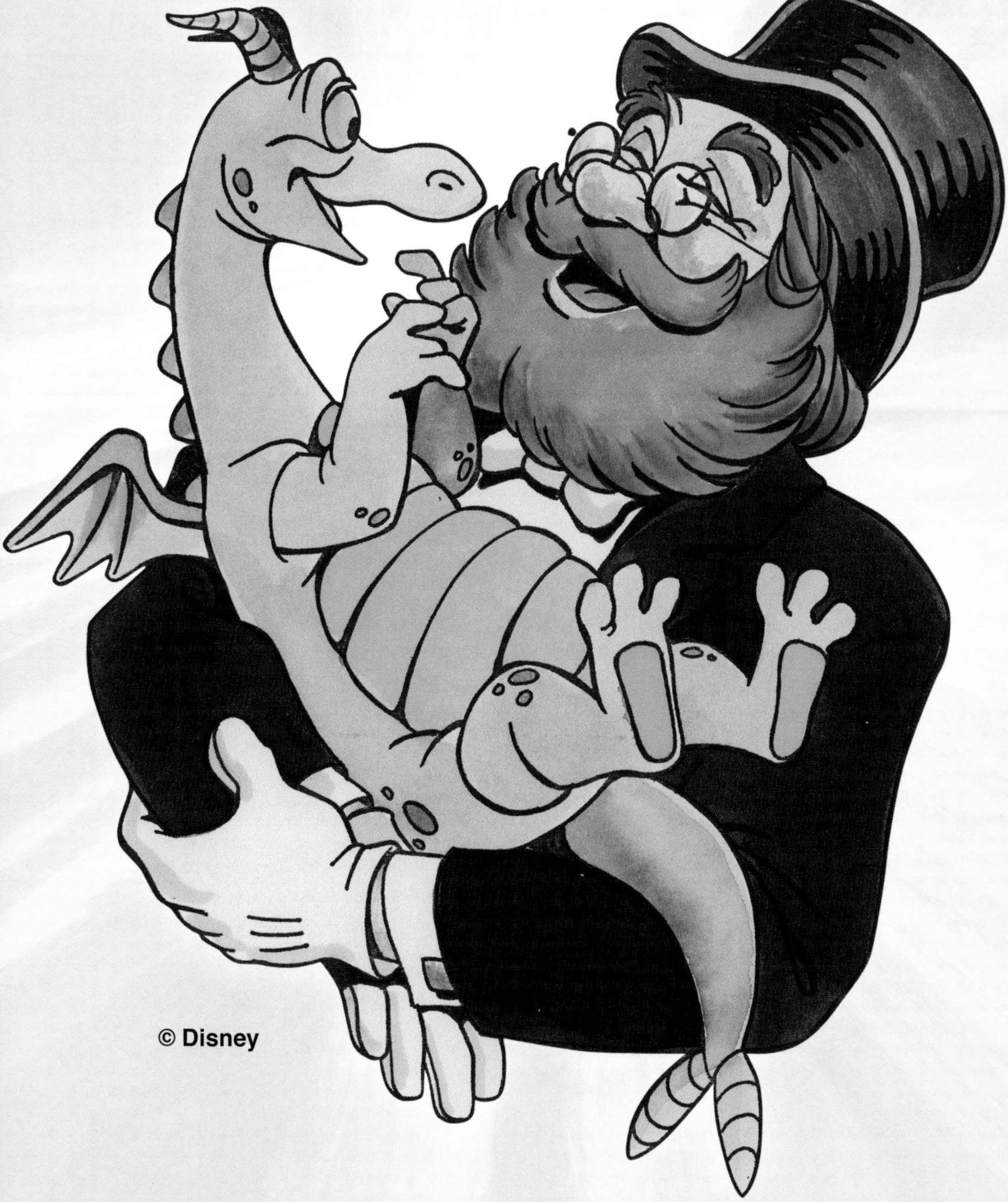
© Disney

Early Figment and Dreamfinder character designs
for the Journey Into Imagination ride by X Atencio

Artwork courtesy of Walt Disney Imagineering Art Collection

FIGMENT 2

Dreamfinder, the legendary inventor from the Academy Scientifica-Lucidus, and **Figment**, his companion, saved the Earth from a destructive force inadvertently unleashed by Dreamfinder's own Integrated Mesmonic Converter. In doing so, the pair traveled from their own time and place in 1910 London through a portal to 21st-century Florida.

There they discovered the Academy has reopened anew, and that in the intervening years their legacy had grown to epic proportions. CHAIRMAN AUCKLEY, head of the new school, doubted the duo's authenticity, but FYE, a sound sprite friend of Figment and Dreamfinder from their first adventure, used his status as professor to vouch for them and give them a chance to address the school with a demonstration. Dreamfinder's self-doubt grew, climaxing with the failure of his invention at the demonstration, which allowed a living Doubt creature hiding inside him to break free and take over his body. The newly formed DOUBTFINDER used his powerful influence to imprison all of the minds at the Academy, squashing creativity to usher in an era of fear and doubt.

Unaffected, Figment fled the Academy in search of help—in search of someone with a spark of creativity powerful enough to defeat the Doubtfinder...

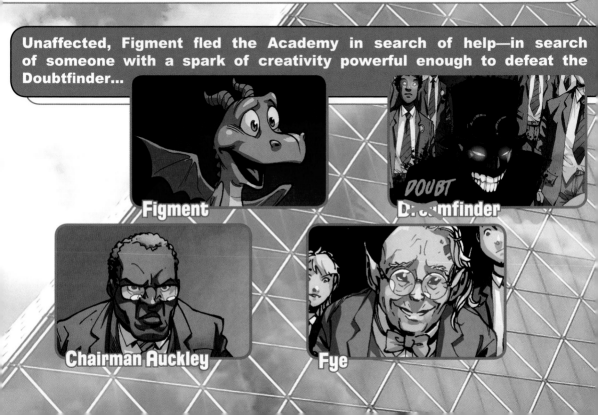

Figment

Dreamfinder

DOUBT

Chairman Auckley

Fye

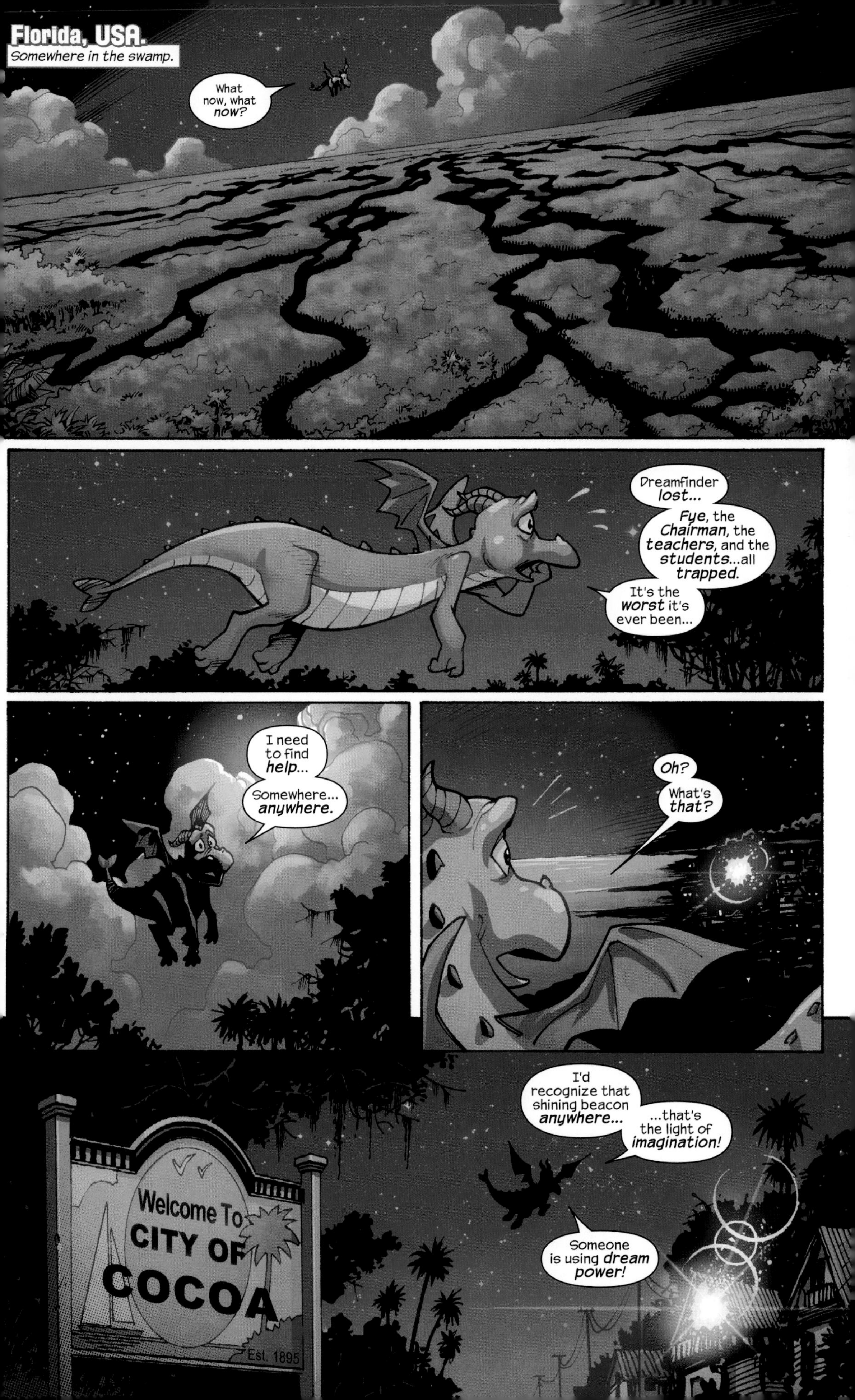
Florida, USA.
Somewhere in the swamp.
What now, what now?
Dreamfinder lost...
Fye, the Chairman, the teachers, and the students...all trapped.
It's the worst it's ever been...
I need to find help...
Somewhere... anywhere.
Oh?
What's that?
I'd recognize that shining beacon anywhere...
...that's the light of imagination!
Someone is using dream power!
Welcome To CITY OF COCOA
Est. 1895

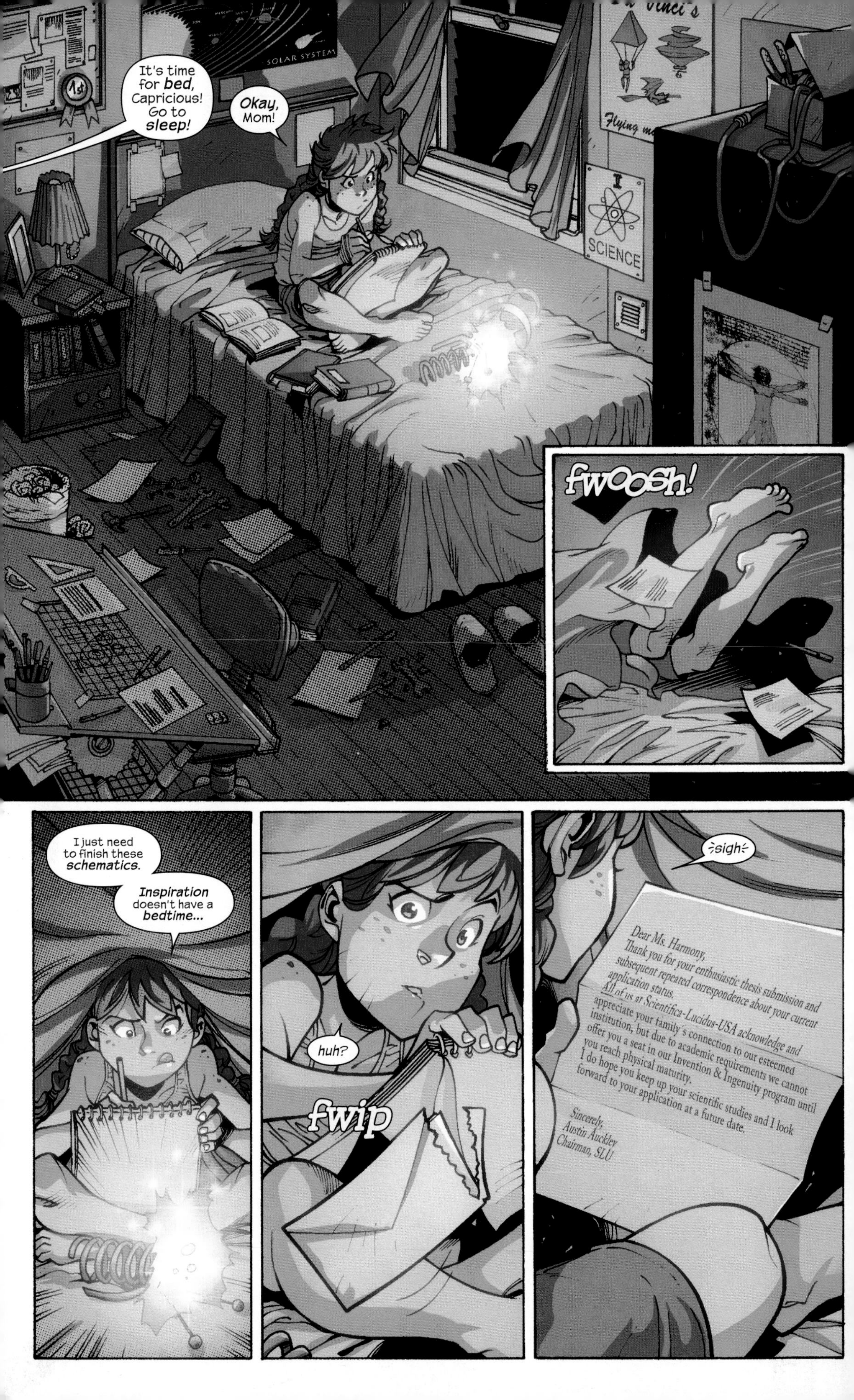
SOLAR SYSTEM
1st
It's time for *bed*, Capricious! Go to *sleep*!
Okay, Mom!
Flying m
SCIENCE
fwoosh!
I just need to finish these *schematics*.
Inspiration doesn't have a *bedtime*...
huh?
fwip
sigh
Dear Ms. Harmony,
Thank you for your enthusiastic thesis submission and subsequent repeated correspondence about your current application status.
All of us at Scientifica-Lucidus-USA acknowledge and appreciate your family's connection to our esteemed institution, but due to academic requirements we cannot offer you a seat in our Invention & Ingenuity program until you reach physical maturity.
I do hope you keep up your scientific studies and I look forward to your application at a future date.
Sincerely,
Austin Auckley
Chairman, SLU

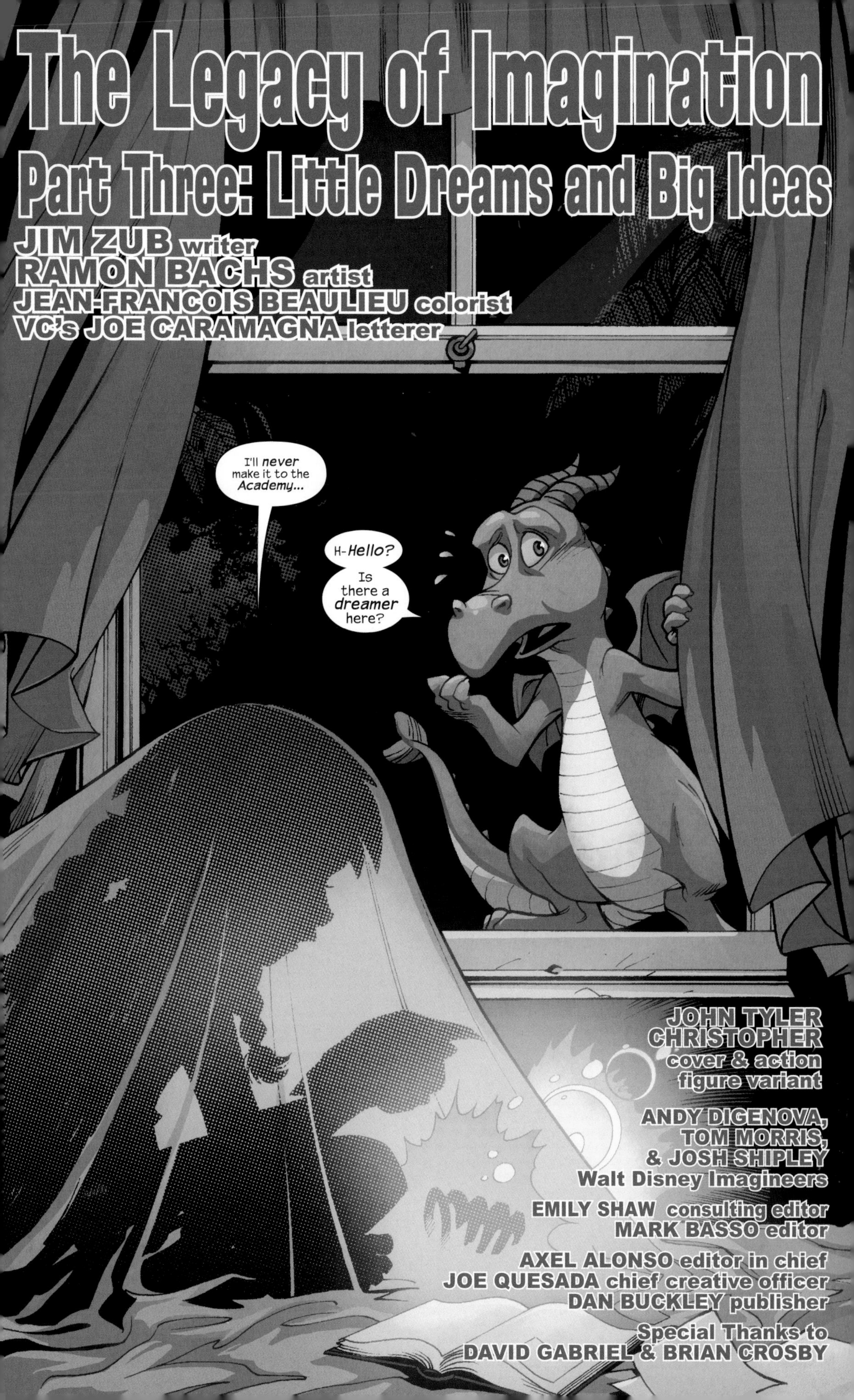
The Legacy of Imagination
Part Three: Little Dreams and Big Ideas
JIM ZUB writer
RAMON BACHS artist
JEAN-FRANCOIS BEAULIEU colorist
VC's JOE CARAMAGNA letterer
I'll never make it to the Academy...
H-Hello? Is there a dreamer here?
JOHN TYLER CHRISTOPHER cover & action figure variant
ANDY DIGENOVA, TOM MORRIS, & JOSH SHIPLEY Walt Disney Imagineers
EMILY SHAW consulting editor
MARK BASSO editor
AXEL ALONSO editor in chief
JOE QUESADA chief creative officer
DAN BUCKLEY publisher
Special Thanks to DAVID GABRIEL & BRIAN CROSBY

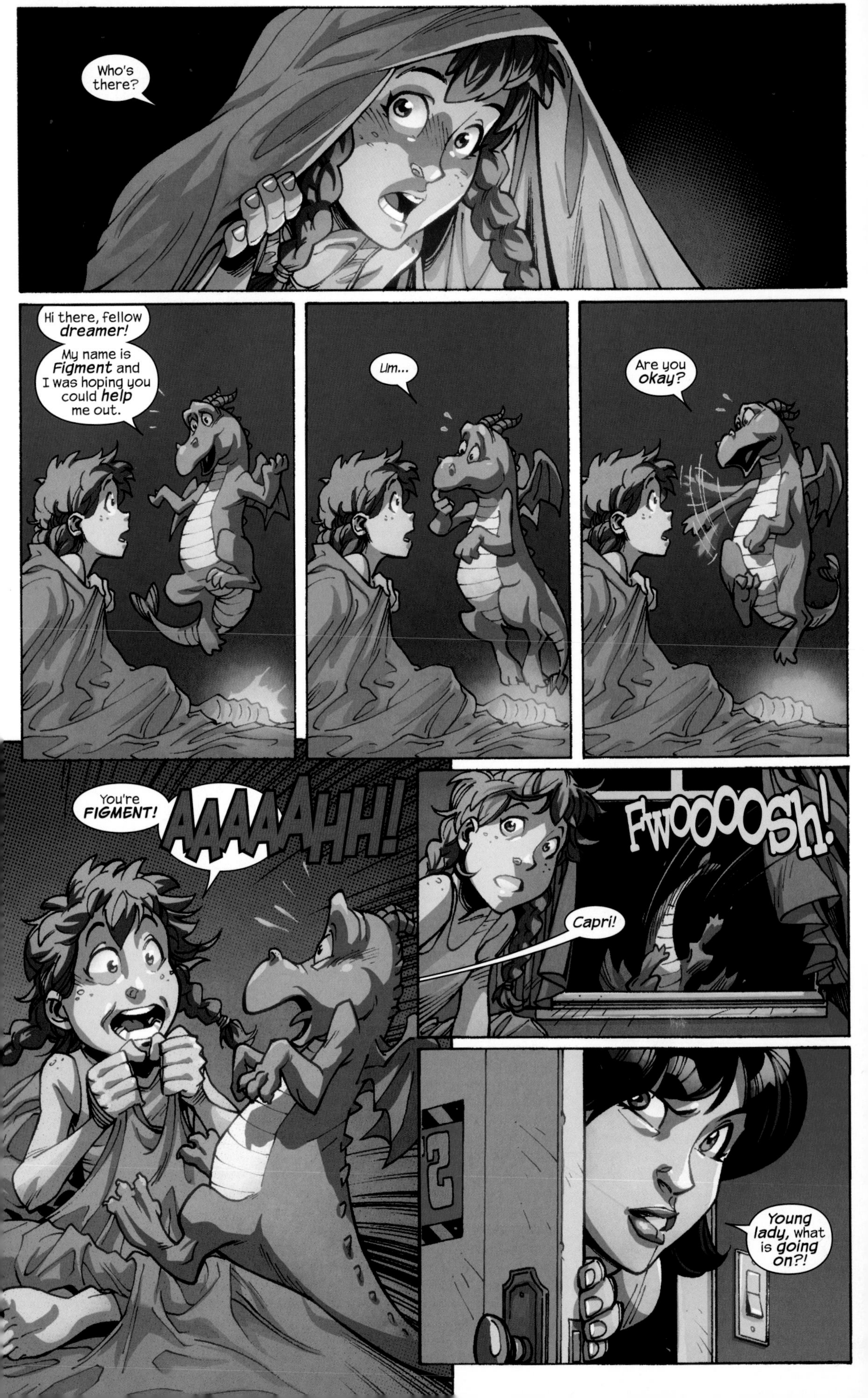
Who's there?
Hi there, fellow dreamer!
My name is Figment and I was hoping you could help me out.
Um...
Are you okay?
You're FIGMENT!
AAAAAHH!
FWOOOOSh!
Capri!
Young lady, what is going on?!

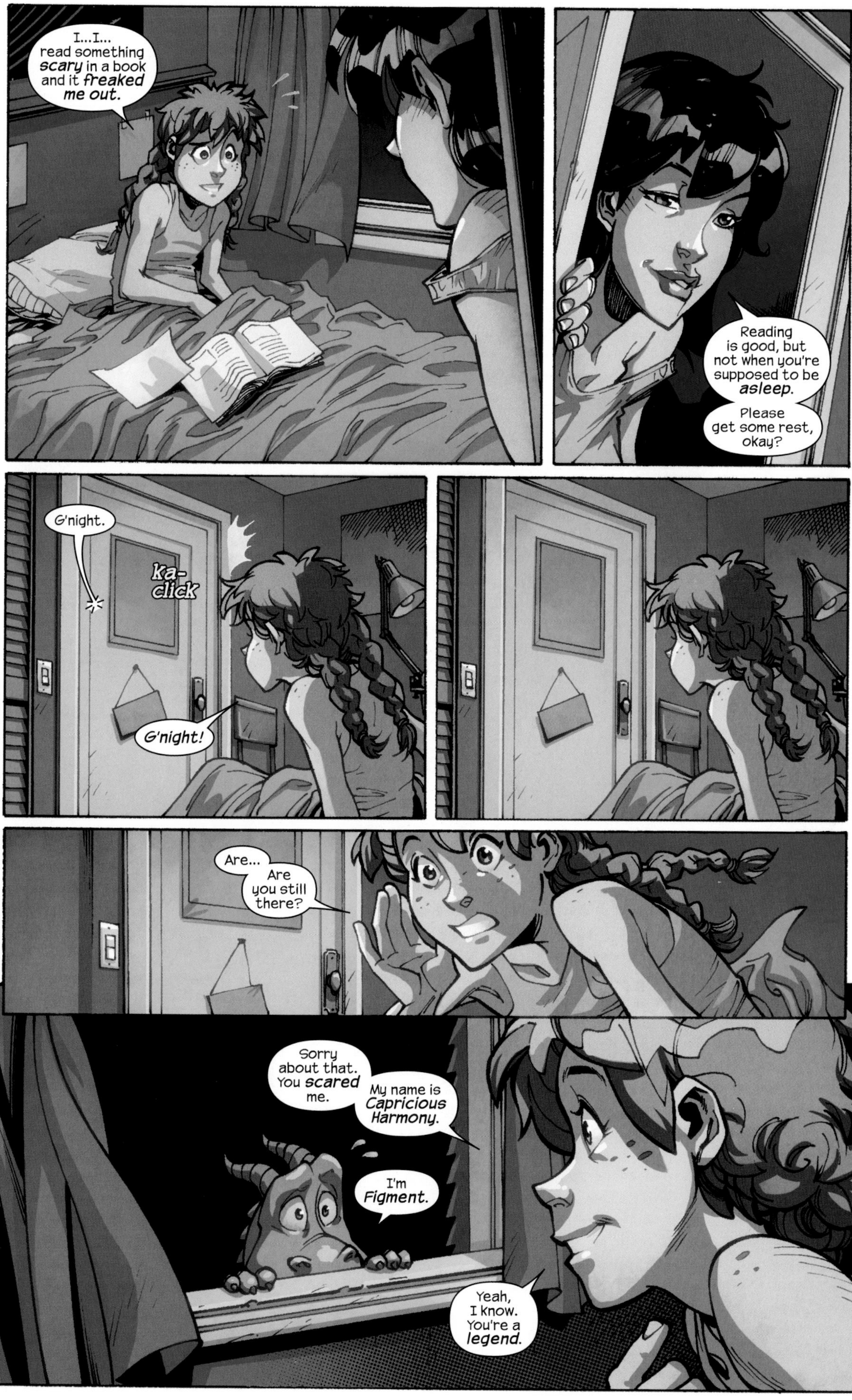
I...I... read something scary in a book and it freaked me out.
Reading is good, but not when you're supposed to be asleep.
Please get some rest, okay?
G'night.
ka-click
G'night!
Are...
Are you still there?
Sorry about that. You scared me.
My name is Capricious Harmony.
I'm Figment.
Yeah, I know. You're a legend.

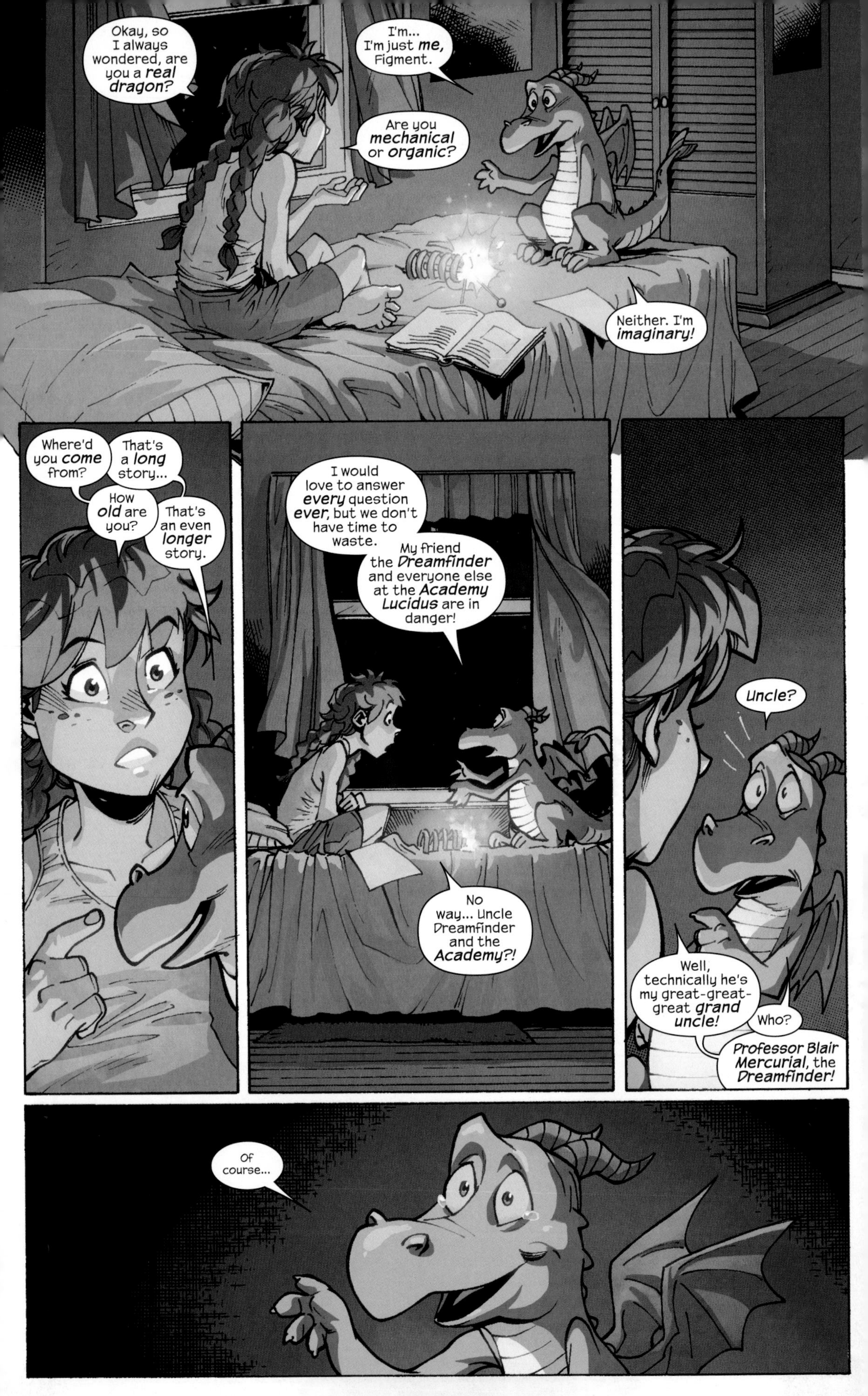
Okay, so I always wondered, are you a real dragon?
I'm... I'm just me, Figment.
Are you mechanical or organic?
Neither. I'm imaginary!
Where'd you come from?
That's a long story...
How old are you?
That's an even longer story.
I would love to answer every question ever, but we don't have time to waste.
My friend the Dreamfinder and everyone else at the Academy Lucidus are in danger!
No way... Uncle Dreamfinder and the Academy?!
Uncle?
Well, technically he's my great-great-great grand uncle!
Who?
Professor Blair Mercurial, the Dreamfinder!
Of course...

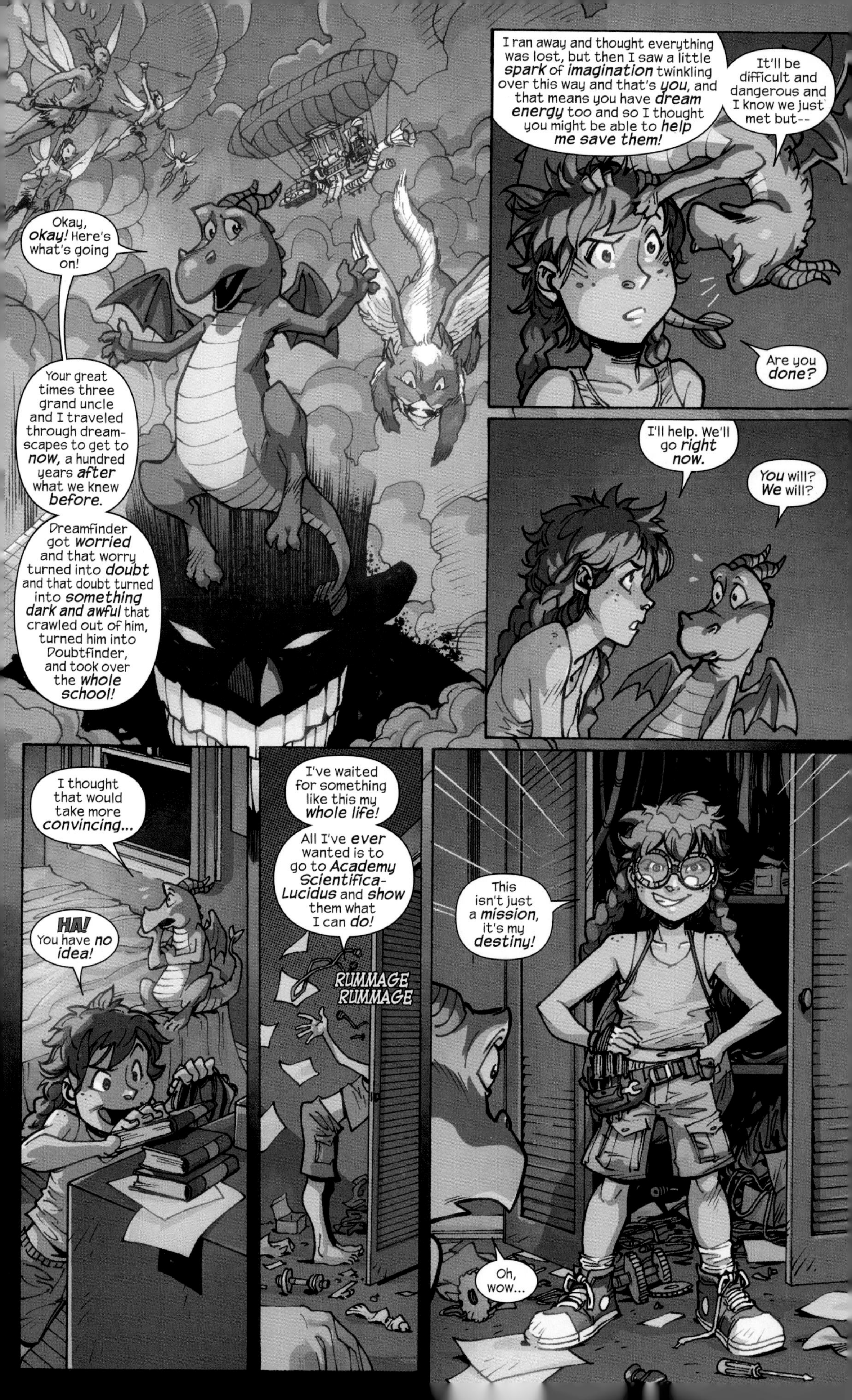
Okay, okay! Here's what's going on!
Your great times three grand uncle and I traveled through dream-scapes to get to now, a hundred years after what we knew before.
Dreamfinder got worried and that worry turned into doubt and that doubt turned into something dark and awful that crawled out of him, turned him into Doubtfinder, and took over the whole school!
I ran away and thought everything was lost, but then I saw a little spark of imagination twinkling over this way and that's you, and that means you have dream energy too and so I thought you might be able to help me save them!
It'll be difficult and dangerous and I know we just met but--
Are you done?
I'll help. We'll go right now.
You will? We will?
I thought that would take more convincing...
HA! You have no idea!
I've waited for something like this my whole life!
All I've ever wanted is to go to Academy Scientifica-Lucidus and show them what I can do!
RUMMAGE RUMMAGE
This isn't just a mission, it's my destiny!
Oh, wow...

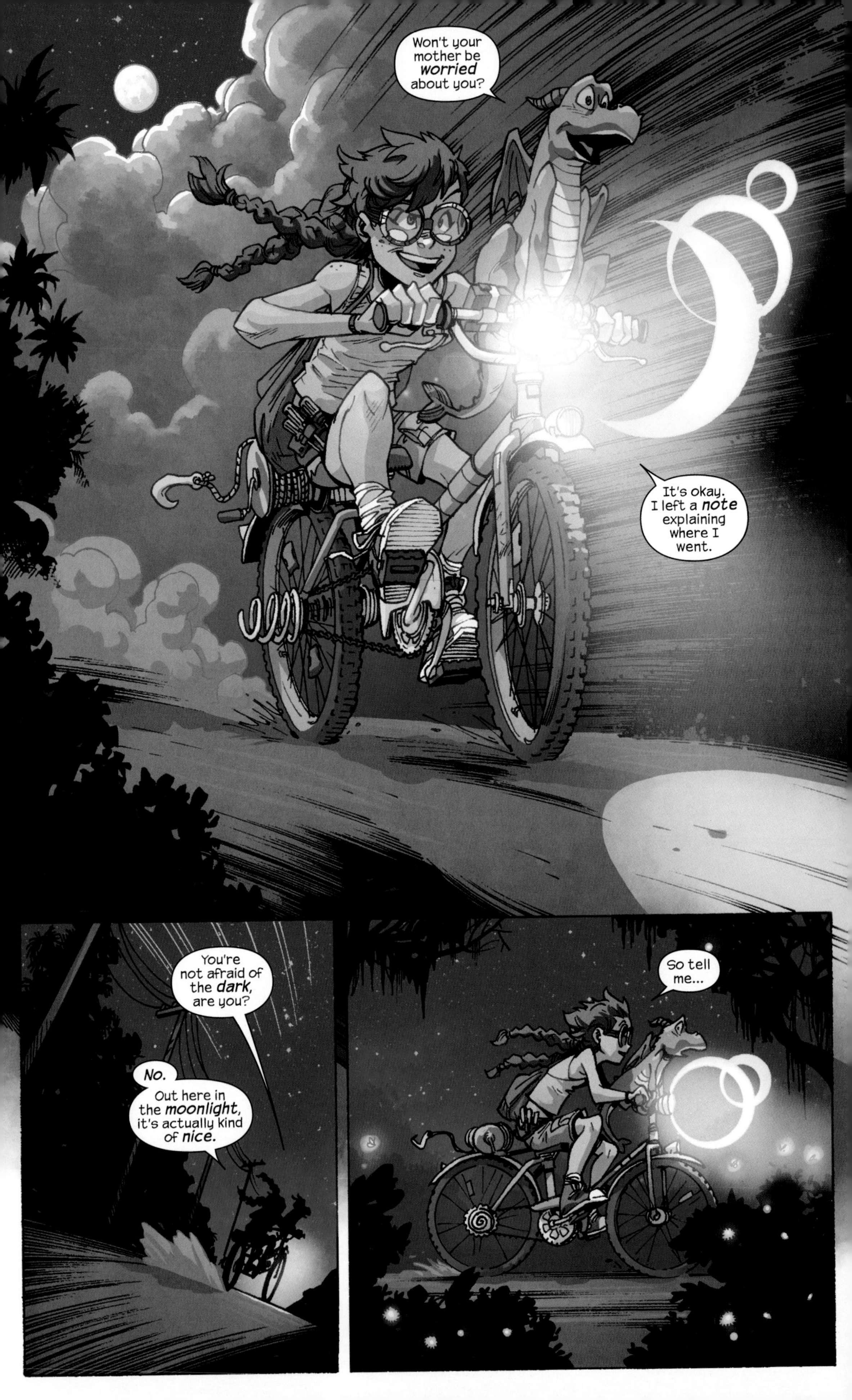
Won't your mother be *worried* about you?
It's okay. I left a *note* explaining where I went.
You're not afraid of the *dark*, are you?
No.
Out here in the *moonlight*, it's actually kind of *nice.*
So tell me...

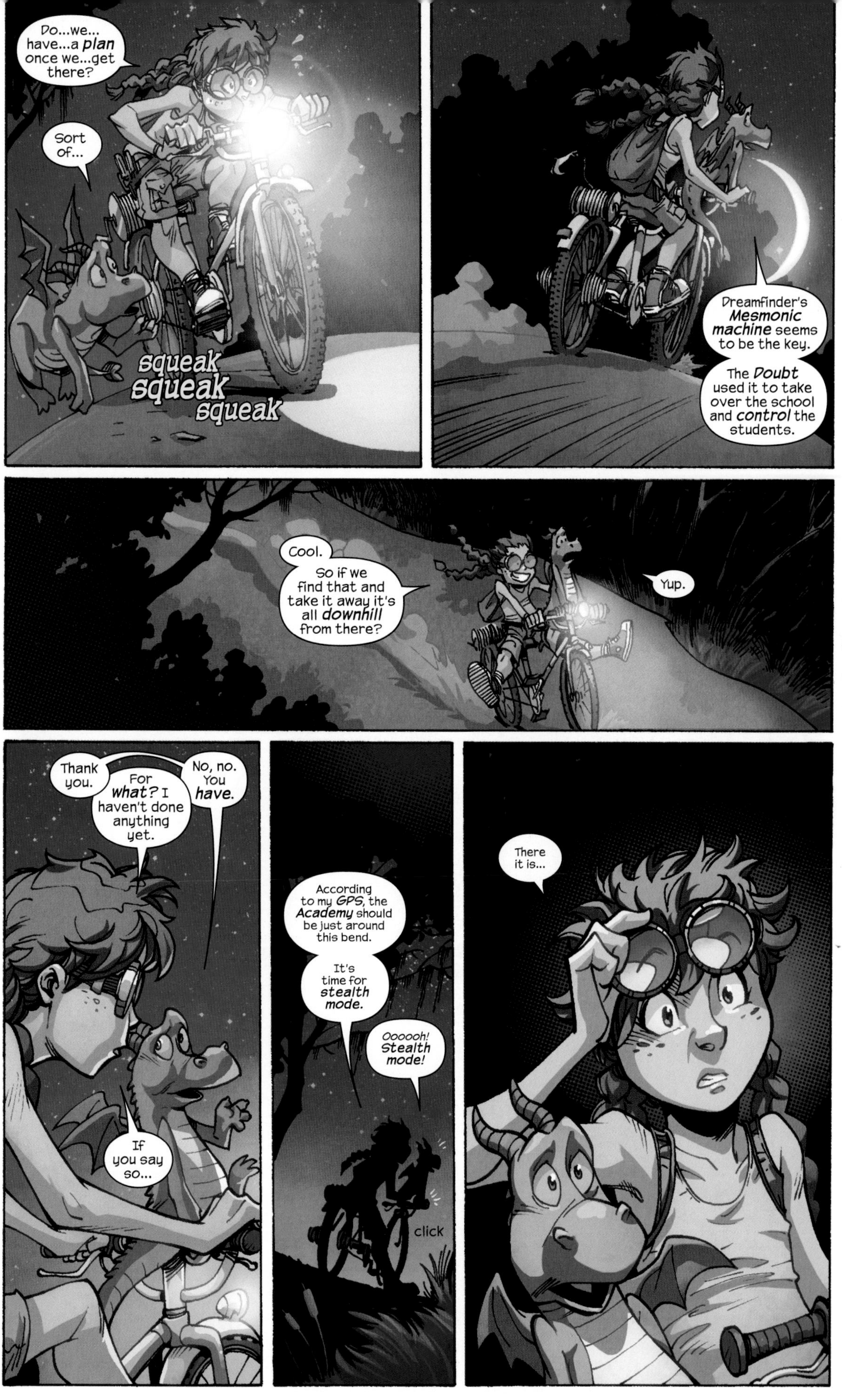

Do...we... have...a plan once we...get there?
Sort of...
squeak squeak squeak
Dreamfinder's Mesmonic machine seems to be the key.
The Doubt used it to take over the school and control the students.
Cool.
So if we find that and take it away it's all downhill from there?
Yup.
Thank you.
For what? I haven't done anything yet.
No, no. You have.
If you say so...
According to my GPS, the Academy should be just around this bend.
It's time for stealth mode.
Oooooh! Stealth mode!
click
There it is...

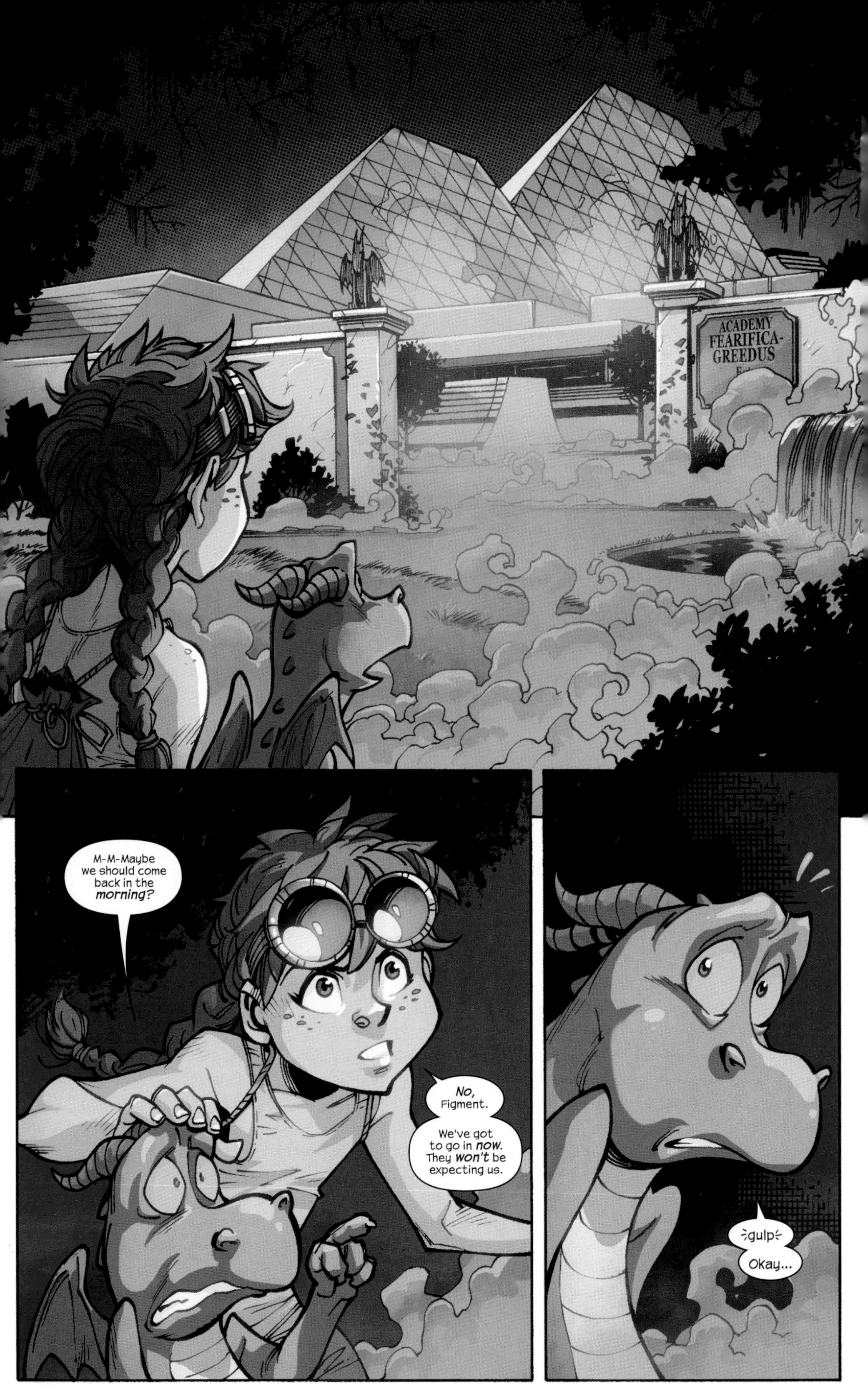
ACADEMY
FEARIFICA-
GREEDUS
M-M-Maybe we should come back in the *morning*?
No, Figment.
We've got to go in ***now***. They ***won't*** be expecting us.
gulp
Okay...

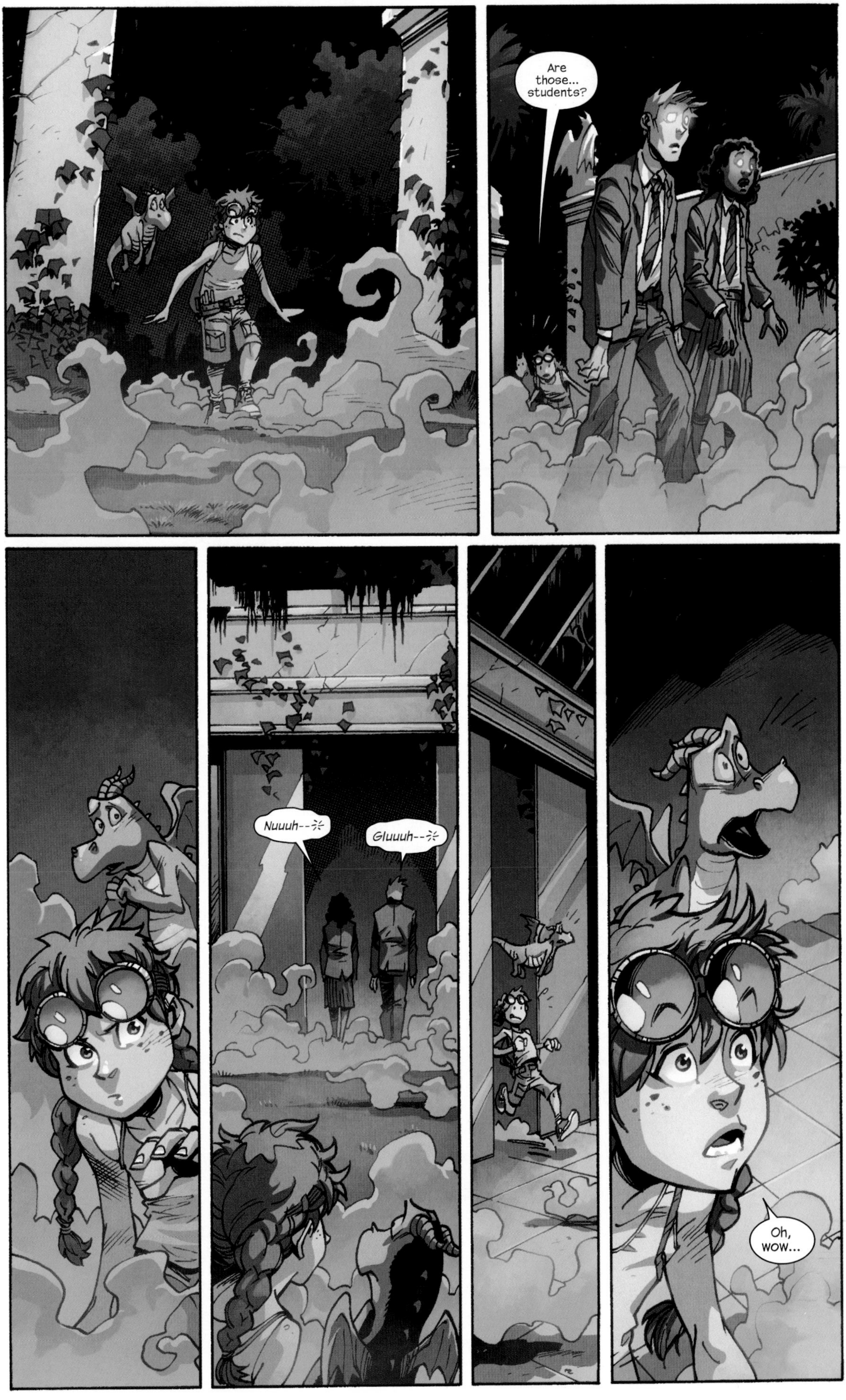
Are those... students?
Nuuuh--
Gluuuh--
Oh, wow...

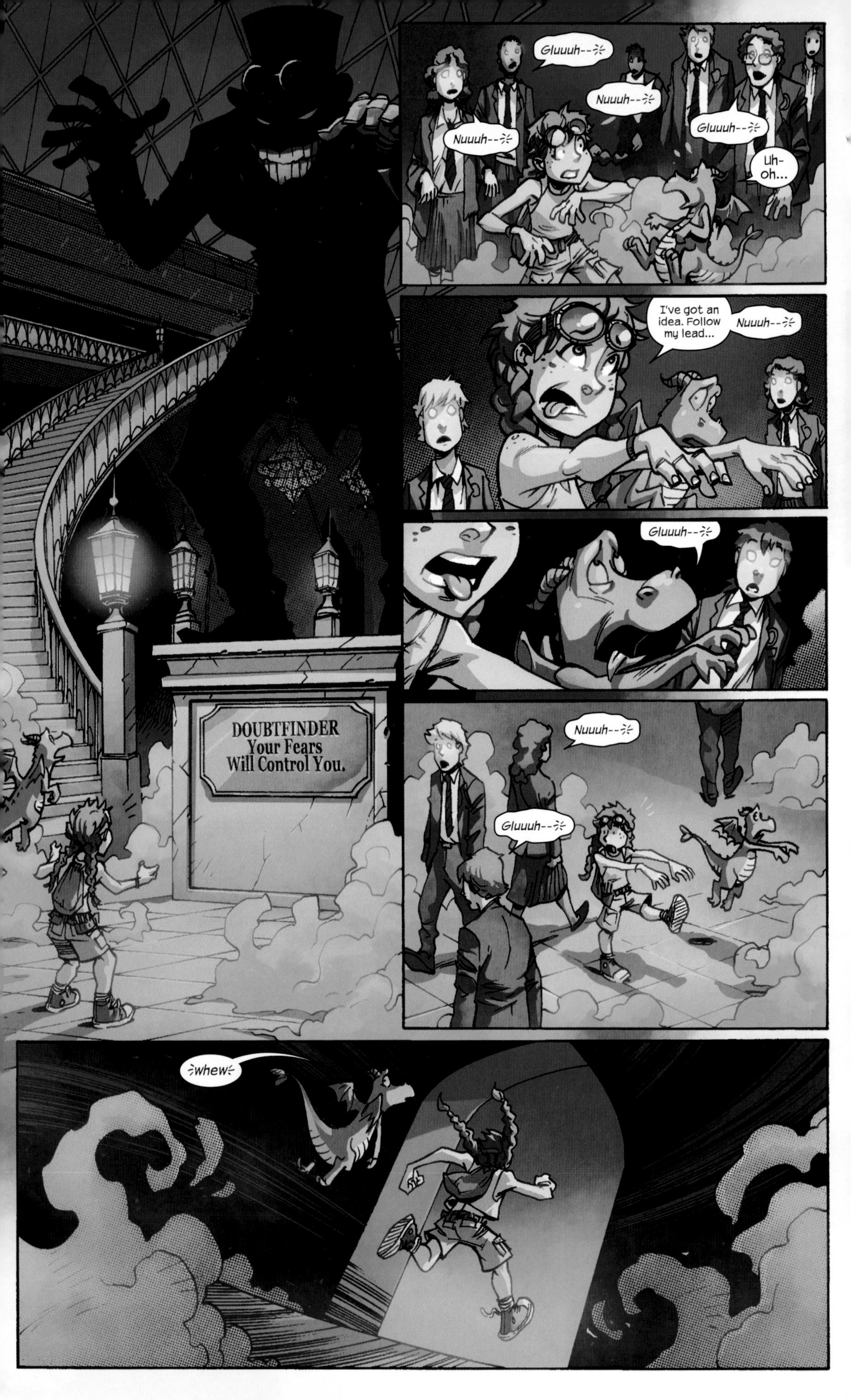
Gluuuh--
Nuuuh--
Nuuuh--
Gluuuh--
Uh-oh...
DOUBTFINDER Your Fears Will Control You.
I've got an idea. Follow my lead...
Nuuuh--
Gluuuh--
Nuuuh--
Gluuuh--
whew

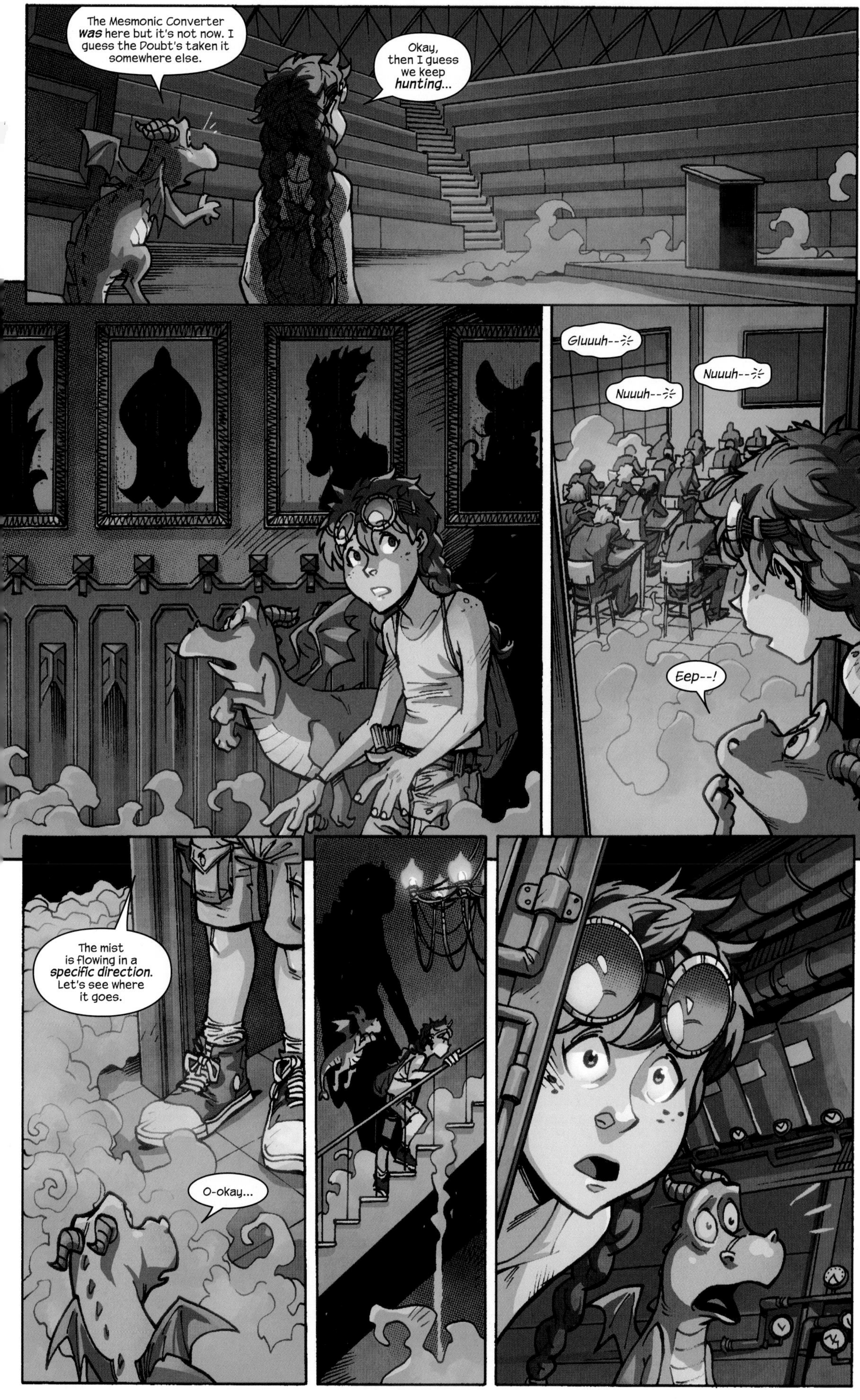
The Mesmonic Converter *was* here but it's not now. I guess the Doubt's taken it somewhere else.
Okay, then I guess we keep *hunting*...
Gluuuh--
Nuuuh--
Nuuuh--
Eep--!
The mist is flowing in a *specific direction*. Let's see where it goes.
O-okay...

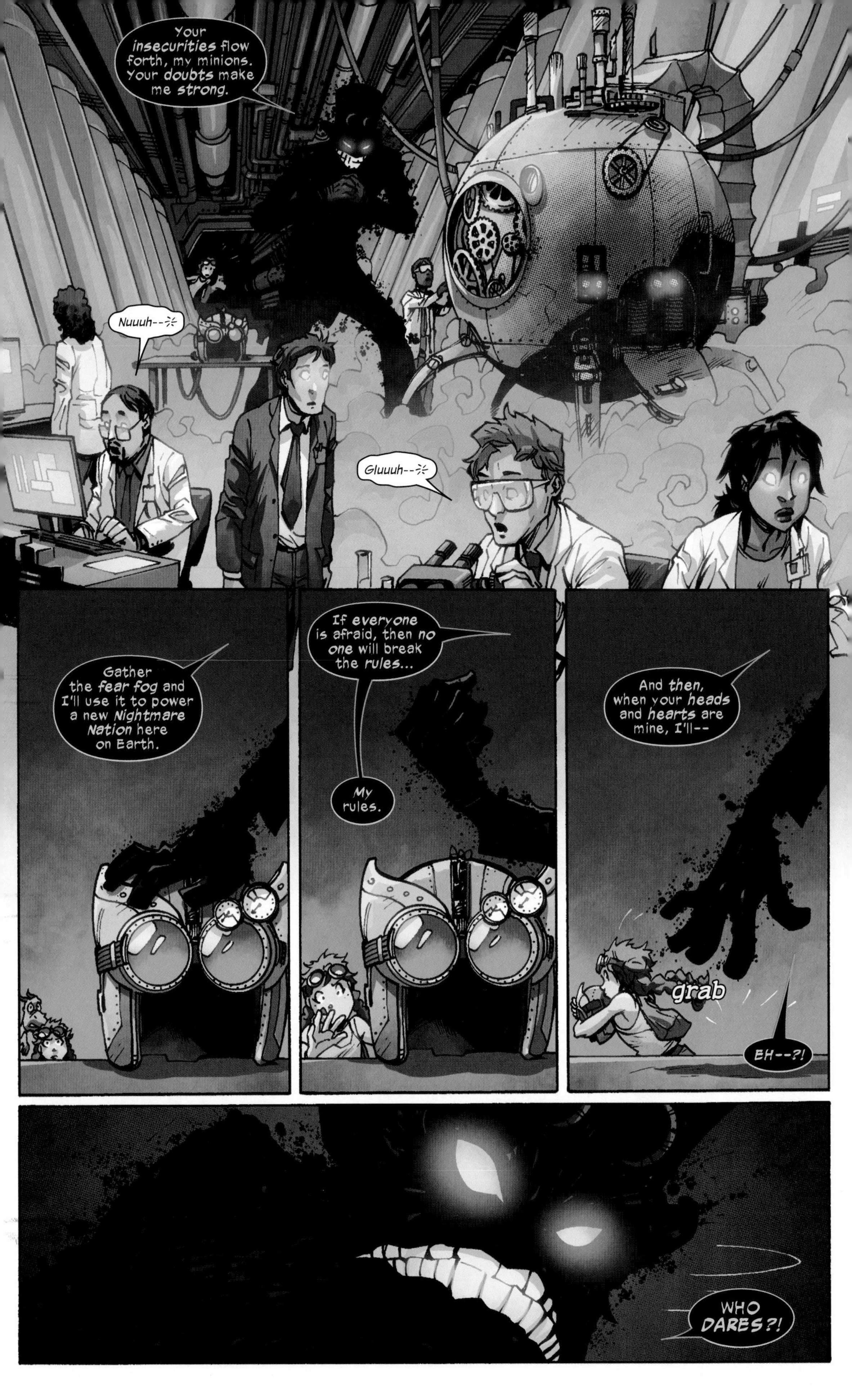
Your insecurities flow forth, my minions. Your doubts make me strong.
Nuuuh--
Gluuuh--
Gather the fear fog and I'll use it to power a new Nightmare Nation here on Earth.
If everyone is afraid, then no one will break the rules...
My rules.
And then, when your heads and hearts are mine, I'll--
grab
EH--?!
WHO DARES?!

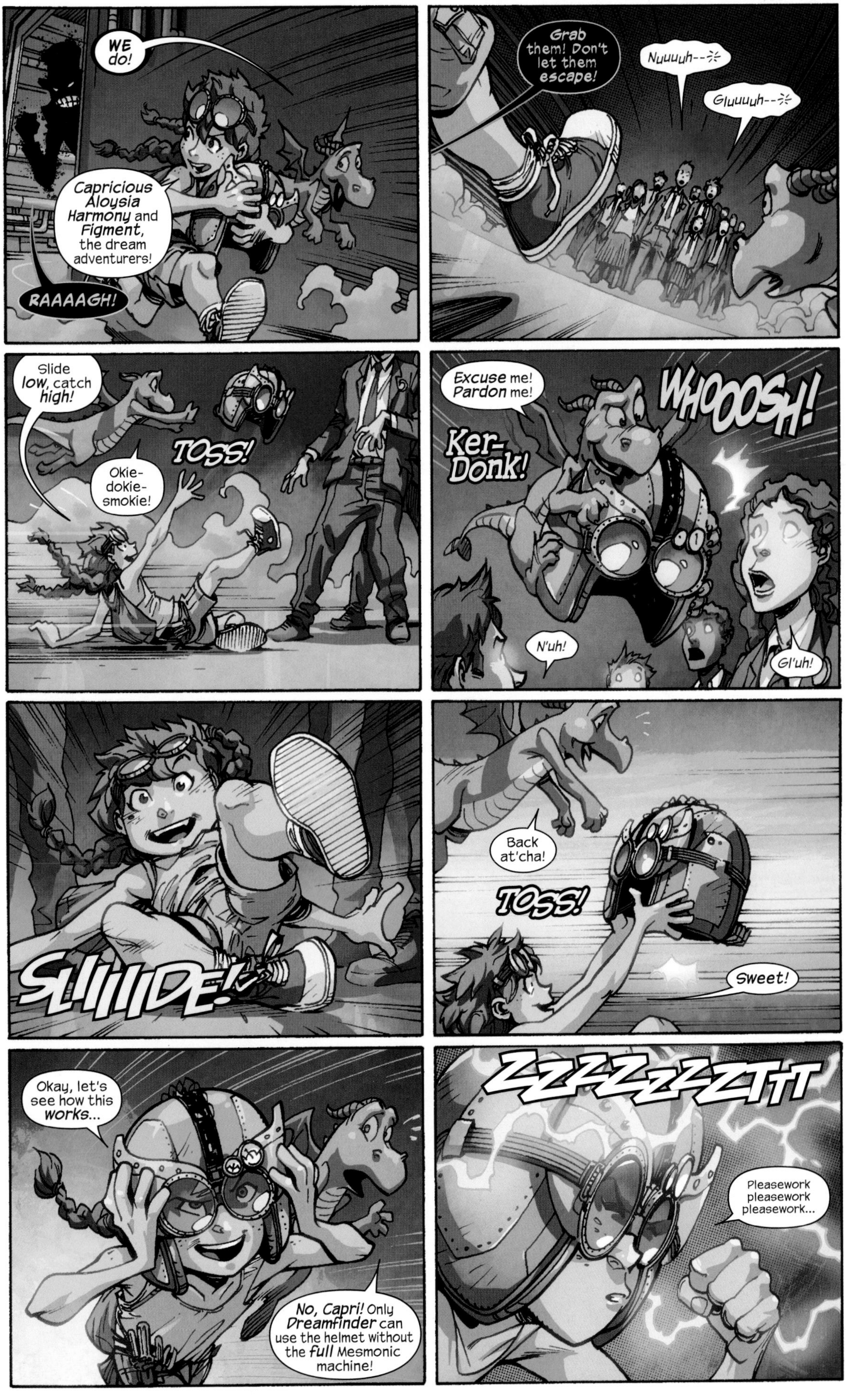
WE do!
Capricious Aloysia Harmony and Figment, the dream adventurers!
RAAAAGH!
Grab them! Don't let them escape!
Nuuuuh--
Gluuuuh--
Slide low, catch high!
Okie-dokie-smokie!
TOSS!
Excuse me! Pardon me!
WHOOOSH!
Ker-Donk!
N'uh!
Gl'uh!
SLIIIIIDE!
Back at'cha!
TOSS!
Sweet!
Okay, let's see how this works...
No, Capri! Only Dreamfinder can use the helmet without the full Mesmonic machine!
ZZZZzzzZTTT
Pleasework pleasework pleasework...

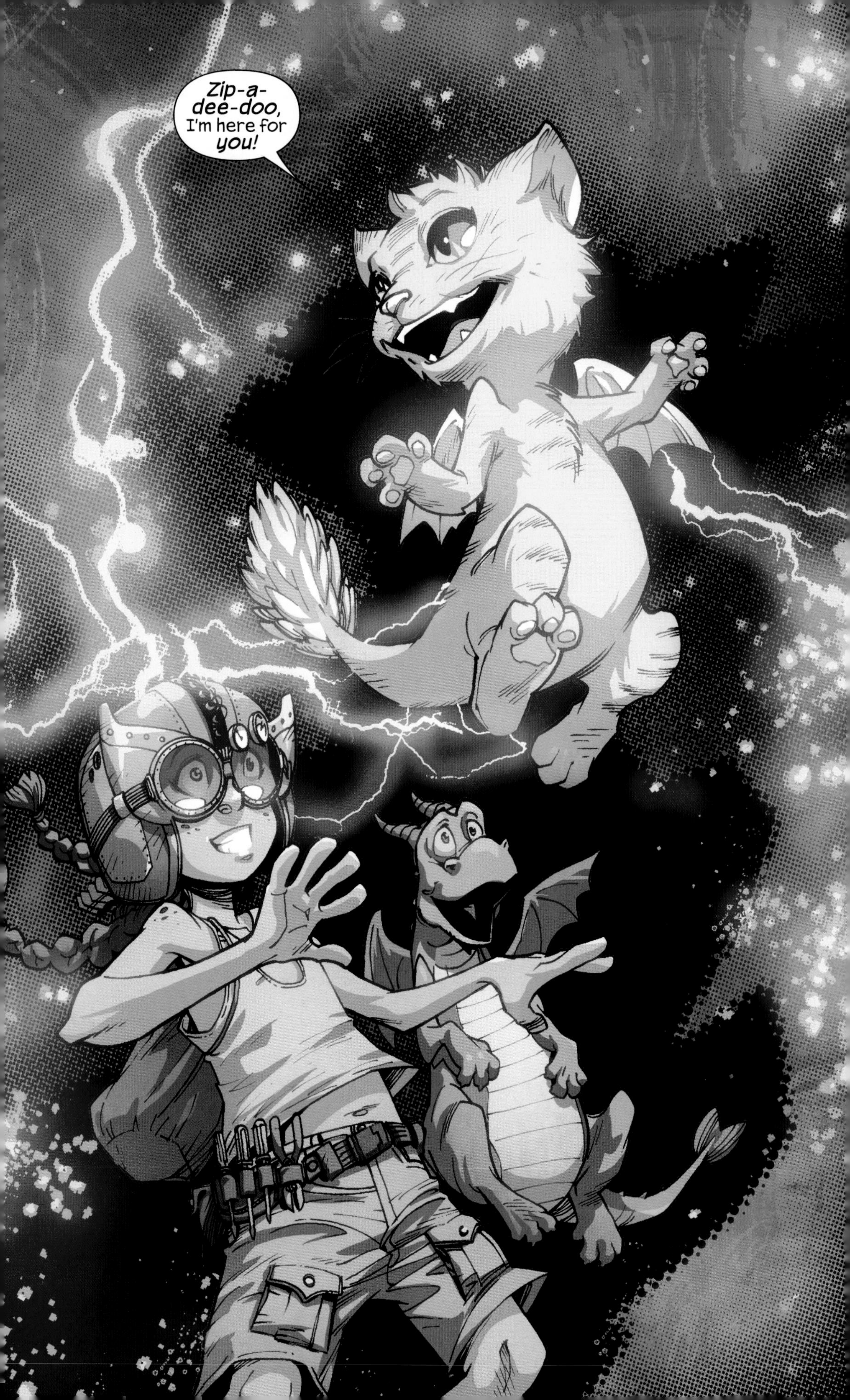
Zip-a-dee-doo, I'm here for you!

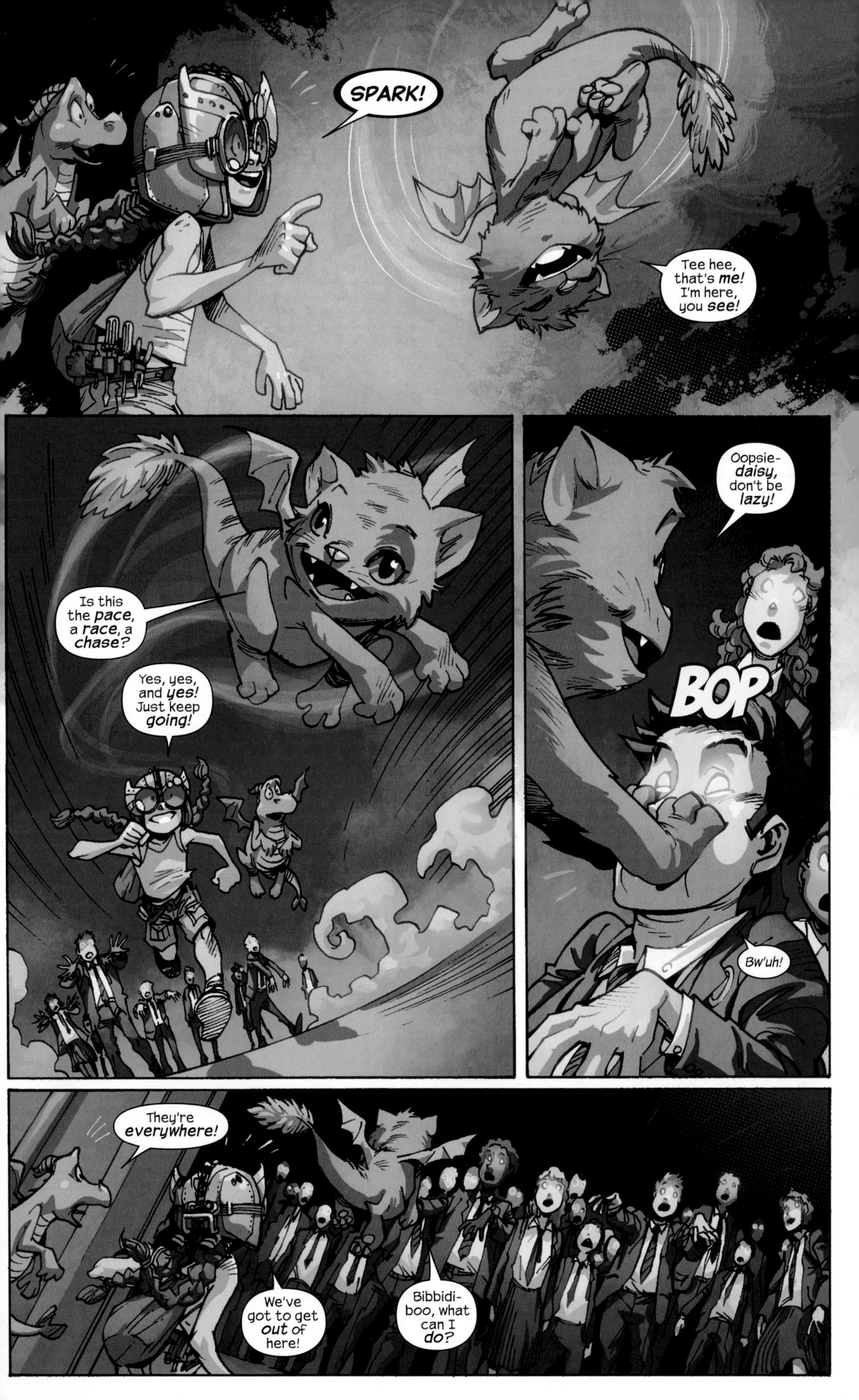
SPARK!
Tee hee, that's *me!* I'm here, you *see!*
Is this the *pace*, a *race*, a *chase?*
Yes, yes, and *yes!* Just keep *going!*
Oopsie-*daisy,* don't be *lazy!*
BOP
Bw'uh!
They're *everywhere!*
We've got to get *out* of here!
Bibbidi-boo, what can I *do?*

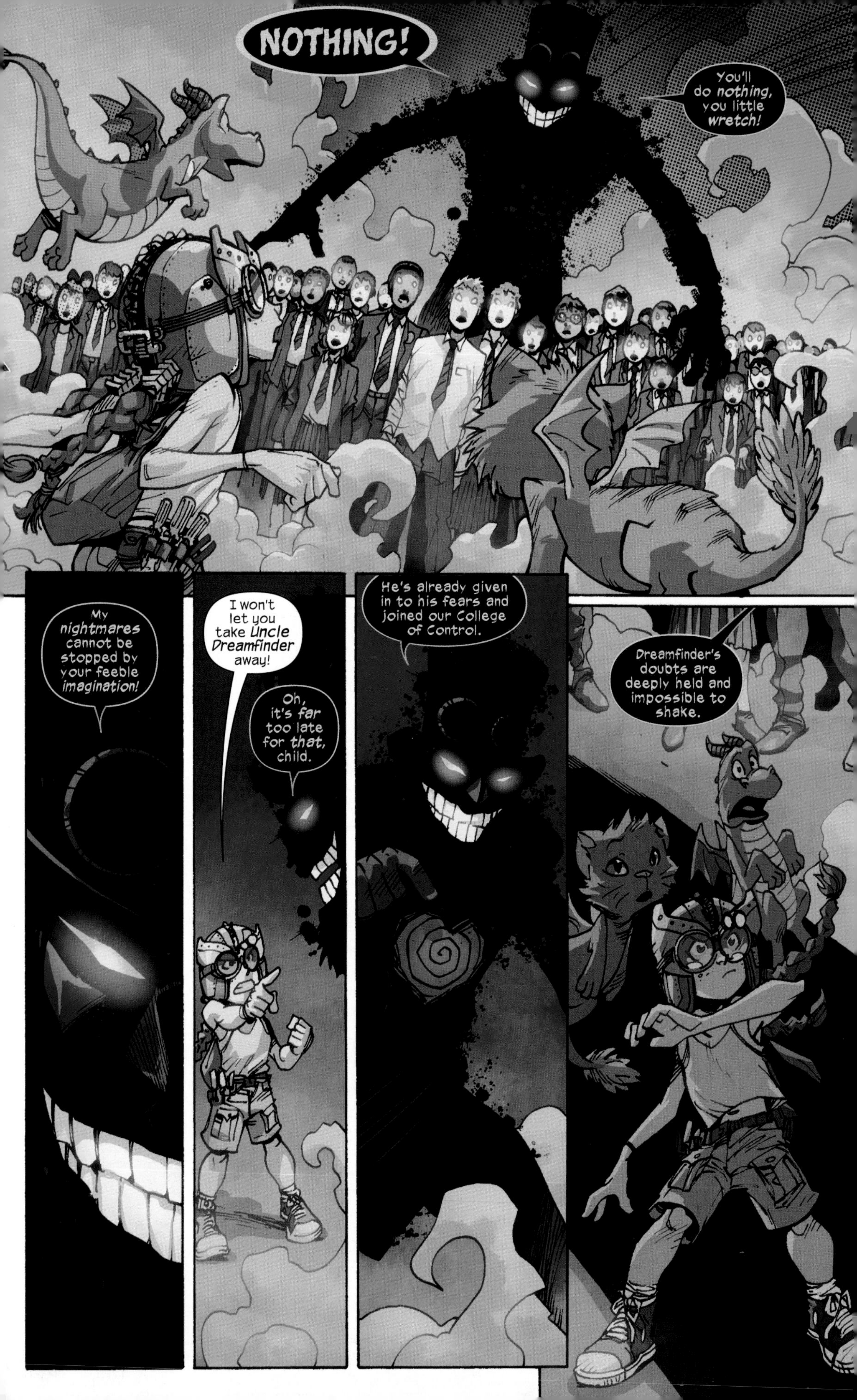
NOTHING!
You'll do nothing, you little wretch!
My nightmares cannot be stopped by your feeble imagination!
I won't let you take Uncle Dreamfinder away!
Oh, it's far too late for that, child.
He's already given in to his fears and joined our College of Control.
Dreamfinder's doubts are deeply held and impossible to shake.

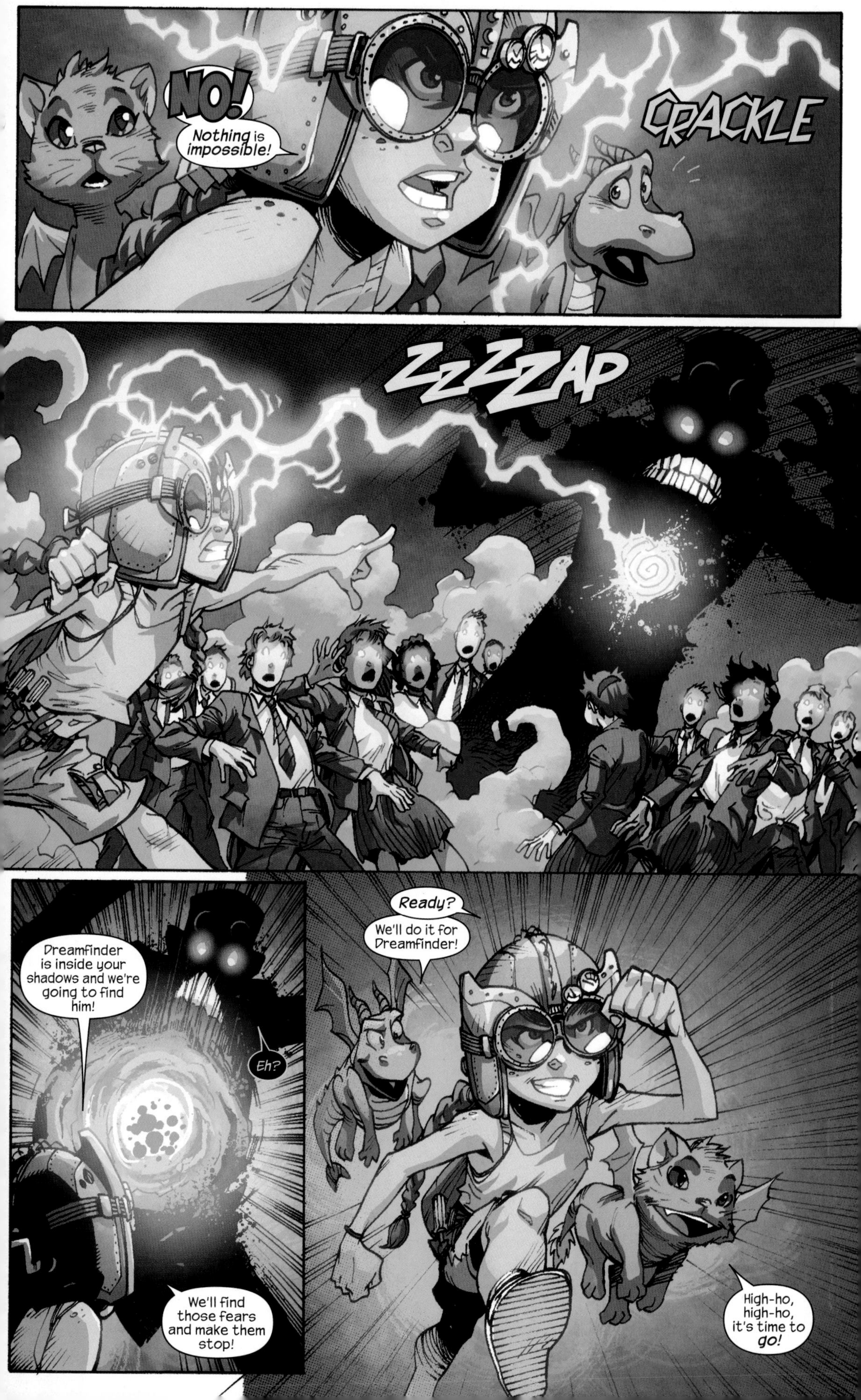
NO!
Nothing is impossible!
CRACKLE
ZZZZAP
Dreamfinder is inside your shadows and we're going to find him!
Eh?
We'll find those fears and make them stop!
Ready?
We'll do it for Dreamfinder!
High-ho, high-ho, it's time to go!

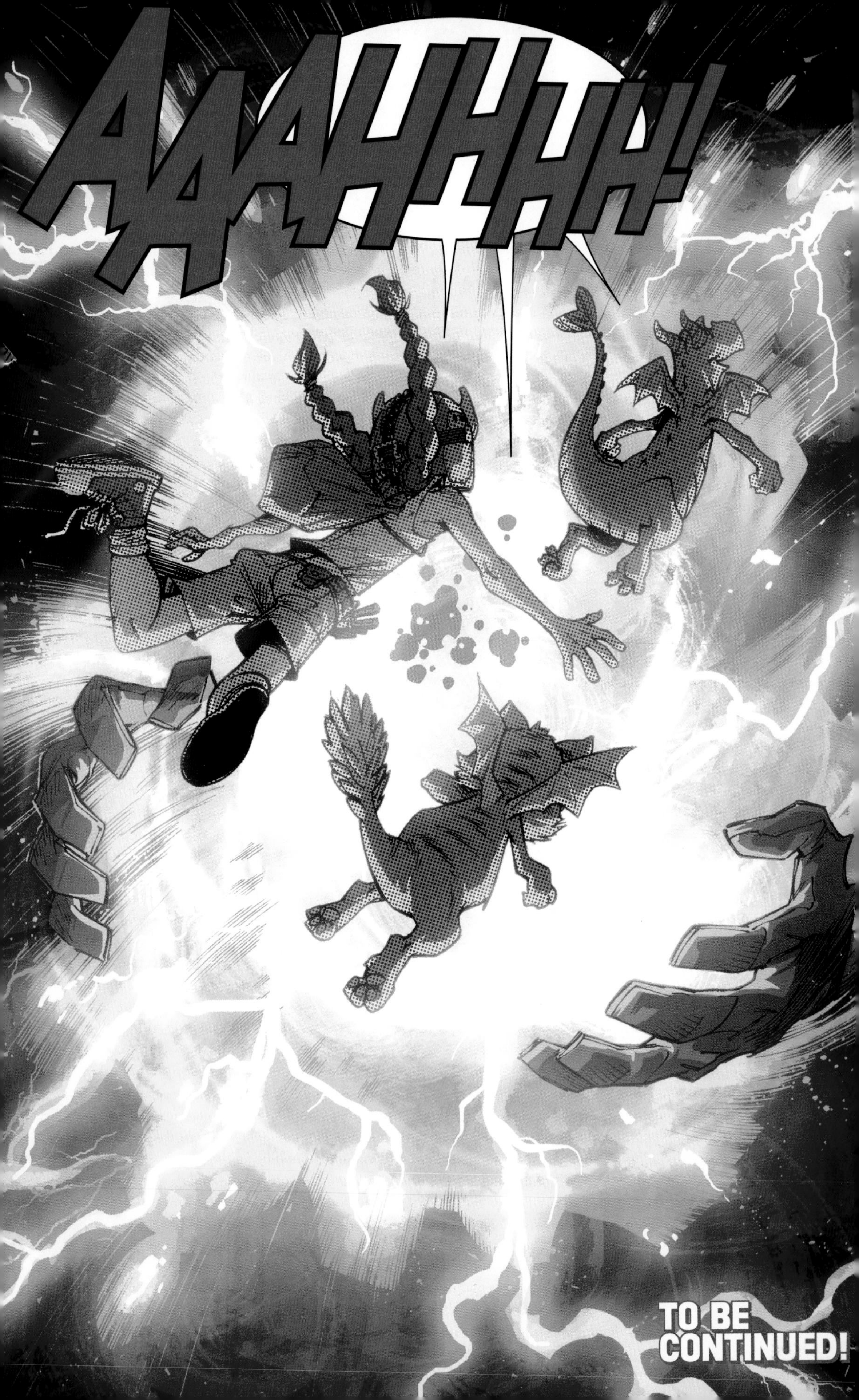
AAAAHHHHH!
TO BE
CONTINUED!